The ADVENTURES of the PRAIRIE-PAXTON FAMILY The Lesson

written by Mary Jane Huckleberry
& illustrated by Marcia Lynes

To order additional copies of this book, contact:
Xlibris
1-888-795-4274
www.Xlibris.com
Orders@Xlibris.com

ISBN: Softcover   978-1-7960-5862-8
        EBook   978-1-7960-5861-1

Print information available on the last page

Rev. date: 06/29/2020

The ADVENTURES of the PRAIRIE-PAXTON FAMILY

The Lesson

 that is my game!" shouted Murphy.

"Nut—you gave that to me last week, said it was a stupid game for babies and I could keep the dumb game!" yelled Kevin.

"I did not!" Murphy yelled back.

"Yes, you did!" Kevin started to yell,

but Momma slipped her head in the room and said the game belonged to her and Dad, and if they could not play nice, then she would take the game so no one could play! Momma said she would be back in the room in

one minute so they needed to decide to play nice or not play the game at all; it was up to them.

Murphy and Kevin sat quietly staring at each other for thirty seconds, then Murphy asked Kevin quietly if he wanted to play the game, so by the time Momma stuck her head back into the room, they were sitting across from each other on the floor, cross-legged, setting up the game between them!

omma smiled and secretly wished all her problems today could be handled so easily, but she wasn't sure that would be possible with her busy schedule today, not so different from every day. But Momma believed that everything always has a way of working itself out, no matter how bad it may seem. If you work hard, keep a smile on your face, and share the love in your heart with those around you, all of your worries will work themselves out. And the strange part is that for Momma, this seems to work because mysteriously by the end of each day, she and Dad have worked together to get everything on their daily list accomplished and they fall asleep peacefully, without a care in the world. Or at least that is always what it seemed like to all of us kids.

By the way, my name is Pauli., and these are the adventures of my family, better known in Prairie Dog Village as the Prairie-Paxton family. We have a total of seventeen in our family, which is large in comparison to most families in our neighborhood, but for the most part, I love being a part of a large family:

my Father (John Prairie-Paxton), Momma (Julie Prairie-Paxton), and a total of fifteen brothers and sisters.

John Jr.and Julie Jr. are twins and are fifteen years old.

Brian, Becka, and
Braden are the triplets now
fourteen years old.

I (Pauli) am twelve.
Sammy and Susie (more
twins) are eleven.

Jacob, Josh, and
Jersey (second set
of triplets) are nine,
and the last two sets of

twins are Murphy and
Missy, seven years old,
and Katie and Kevin,
who are five.

We live at 15 plus 2 Dust Road, in the large hole house at the end of the block, and I know what you are thinking. In the human world, this would be a strange address, but in our dog cities, it's pretty normal. And just so you know, the "plus 2" means that we took two holes and made it into one home, which Dad said was really smart and much cheaper than starting to dig a brand-new bigger hole in a new location.

We are a pretty close-knit family who, for the most part, do a lot of stuff together—well, normally in groups of four or five but we all look out for each other. Don't get me wrong; we have our normal family squabbles as to whose turn it is to take out the trash, who was playing with what toy first, but all in all, we make up a normal happy prairie-dog family.

As the middle dog and the only one of the siblings who is not a twin or triplet, there are times I feel alone even in our big family, and feel that may be the reason I always seem to get into trouble, although most of the time it really is not my fault. I just seem to have bad luck and always seem to be in the wrong place at the wrong time.

Like the time last week when I went to the store to pick up some lettuce for Mom. The whole pile of lettuce fell to the floor right in front of my paws because the little p-dog before me decided the bottom lettuce was best and ran away before Mr. Prairie-Sanders, the store clerk, saw him, so I had to stay and pick up the lettuce mess even though it was not my fault.

Well, on this particular day, I was not feeling well, so Mom decided it was best for me to stay home from school, which made me very happy because I think we go to school too many days as it is. School should only be one or two days a week, not five, so I was very happy to stay home and get the special attention from Momma.

I took my blanket and settled in on the couch to watch cartoons while Momma made me toast and tea and Dad came in to give me a hug goodbye before he left for work.

What a good day this was going to be, even though my tummy was a little upset!

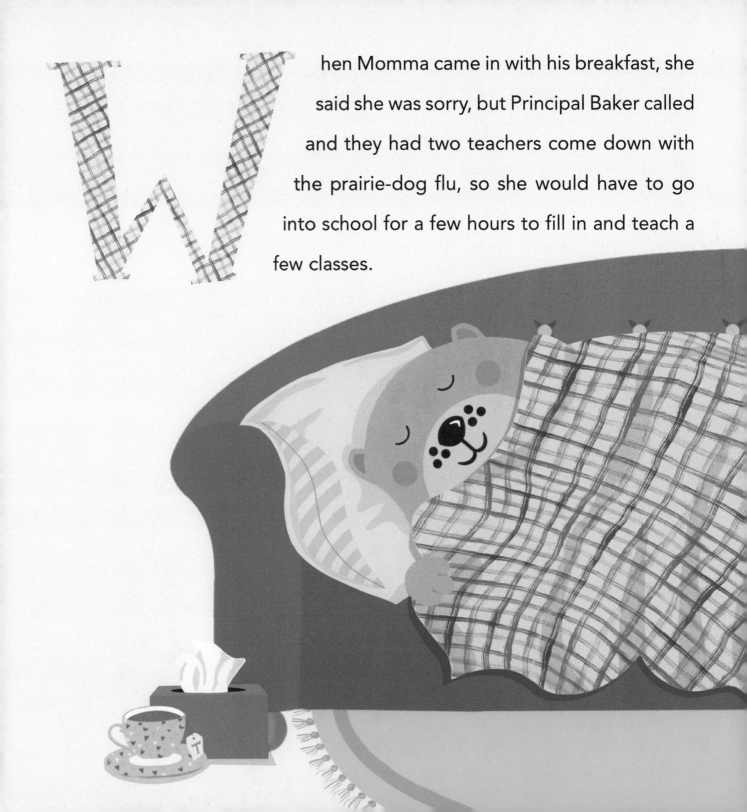

When Momma came in with his breakfast, she said she was sorry, but Principal Baker called and they had two teachers come down with the prairie-dog flu, so she would have to go into school for a few hours to fill in and teach a few classes.

(Mom used to be a full-time teacher but is now a full-time mom and fills in at the school when needed.) But she said that she would be back home by 1:00 p.m., and to stay on the couch, and she would be back home before he knew it.

I was not happy to hear the news, but a little while after Mom left, I thought it was kinda neat to be in the house alone.

This never happens with a family of seventeen; you are never alone. So I decided it would be a good chance to play with some of John Jr's cool stuff. I never get to when he is home annnndddddd it is OK to borrow every once in a while. *Even though I should ask, there is no one here to ask, so if I take real good care of what I borrow and put it back before anyone comes home, no one will ever know.*

So I went straight to John Jr.'s chest in the corner of our room, at the end of John Jr.'s bed, and pulled out John Jr.'s brand-new handheld video game that I had been dying to play. John Jr. had worked hard to save for over six months to buy the game himself. *Besides, Momma did tell me to stay down on the couch.* And I could definitely stay down for hours while playing the game, so I was doing what Momma told me to do, and only following instructions..

I had a good ol' time playing the video game and put it back in John Jr.'s chest just before Momma got home from school. It turned out to be a great morning even though I was still feeling a little sick. I really thought I would be scared of being alone, but it was really kinda cool and wished I could do it more often.

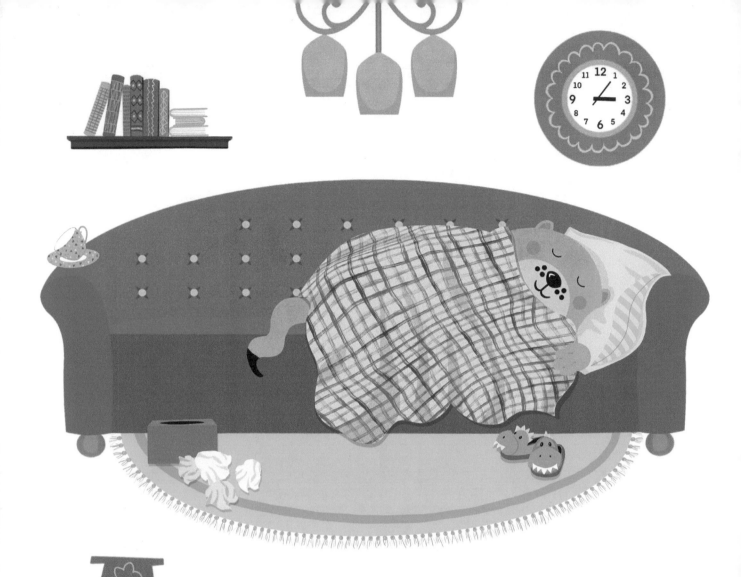

At a little after three o'clock, the rest of the Prairie-Paxton family got home, and they all stopped by to see how I was feeling before going to their rooms to do their homework.

Momma had asked Sammy to stop by my classroom and pick up the day's schoolwork for me so I would not fall behind, which Sammy did, and he gave it to me before going to his room. So I started working on my schoolwork with the rest of the kids, while

Dad sat down to read the *Prairie News* paper and Mom made herself busy in the kitchen.

Everyone finished their homework just before Momma called us all in for

dinner, for my favorite vegetable stew and rhubarb pie for dessert, and we

all raced into the kitchen and jumped in our chairs, ready to say our prayers

before dinner! When Dad came into the room, we all bowed our heads and

waited for him to begin, and after prayer, we all dug in like we had not

eaten in days, even me with my upset stomach, which, after the great day

I had, was beginning to feel so much better! Momma even said that she

was happy to see that I was feeling better, and so was I!

After dinner, we all pitched in to clean up so Mom and Dad could have some of what they called quiet time. Don't know why they like their quiet time so much, sounds kinda boring to me, but they seem to like it. So after the kitchen was clean, John Jr. went to his room to play with his video game. Julie ran to the phone to call her friends, same thing she does every night, which also

seems very boring to me. Murphy, Missy, Katie, and Kevin went down the street to meet some friends, and Brian, Becka, Braden, Sammy, Susie, Jacob, Josh, Jersey, and I went out for a baseball game in the field next to our back-door hole. Momma normally does not let any of us play outside if we stayed home sick from school, but since I did all of my homework so I wouldn't be behind in class, she let me come out for an hour.

Becka was getting ready to bat when John Jr. came out of the house with a weird look on his face, like he was either going to get sick or angry or maybe both; it was hard to tell, but whichever it was, I was pretty sure I didn't want to be next to him when he blew. And just then, I saw the video game in his hand and got a weird feeling in my stomach.

But how could he know I borrowed it? I put it back in his chest before anyone was home. Wait, maybe he is upset about something else. And then I saw the broken screen on the video game. *I better run away now while I have the chance!* I thought.

Just then, John yelled, "OK, who was in my chest? Whoever it was better tell me now, because you moved my video game and it got smashed when the top of the chest closed, so you better fess up because if you don't speak up and I find out who it was, I am going to—"

Just then, Dad came up the hole to see what all the yelling was about, so John Jr. tried to calm down and tell him what happened. When he was done, Dad looked around at all of our faces and stopped when he got to mine. *Oh boy, I'm done for*, I thought, and before Dad could say anything, I cried out, "OK, it was me. I'm sorry. I didn't mean to break it, only borrowed it for a while this afternoon. I was bored and tried to be very careful and didn't know it broke when I shut the top." John Jr. started to run toward me, but Dad stopped him and said, "Stay calm. Nothing is ever solved when you are angry."

IT WAS ME!

Dad asked John Jr. how much the video game cost. He then turned to me after John answered him and said, "You will come to my office to work with me every day after school for the next two months to earn enough money to replace the broken video game, in addition to doing extra chores around the house for Momma and being grounded for the next two weeks."

I was about to protest, but when I saw the look on Dad's face, I knew it wasn't a good idea, so all I said was "Yes, sir," and I turned to John and told him how sorry I was that I borrowed his game without asking and even sorrier that I broke it.

ater that night when Dad and Mom came in to give us our kisses and hugs good night, Momma gave me an extra hug and said that she hoped I had learned my lesson. I answered yes, and she asked what lesson I had learned. I told her that I learned that if I do borrow someone's stuff without asking to make sure to put it back in the same spot I found it in so nothing will happen to it.

Momma sat back and looked at me and said, "Looks like I need to add a few more chores and an extra week of grounding to the sentence Dad already gave you—"

"No, Momma, please, I was just joking! What I really learned was not to ever take things without asking."

"And?" she said.

I said, "Because it is not nice."

And she said, "Why is it not nice?"

I sat quiet for a second then said, "Because it's not nice to go through someone's private stuff when they are not around. I wouldn't want anybody taking my stuff without asking, so I shouldn't do that to anyone else! Did I get it right?" I asked.

"Yes, sweetheart," said Momma, "I believe you got it that time."

When Pauli said his prayers that night, he apologized for disobeying but also gave a big thank-you that he did not borrow John Jr's video camera because if he had broken that, he would be working with Dad after school for a lot longer than two months!

Stay tuned for further adventures with the Prairie-Paxton family!

CPSIA information can be obtained
at www.ICGtesting.com
Printed in the USA
LVHW072139020720
659626LV00016B/1681